Shrews Can't Hoop!?

Ray Nelson, Jr. & Douglas Kelly

For every kid who has ever been picked last.

Flying Rhino Productions, Inc. is a company dedicated to the
education and entertainment of elementary school students.

Flying Rhino Books

The Internal Adventures of Donovan Willoughby
(Health and Anatomy)

Greetings From America
(U.S. Geography)

The Seven Seas of Billy's Bathtub
(Ocean and Sea Life)

Connie and Bonnie's Birthday Blastoff
(Astronomy and the Solar System)

A Dinosaur Ate My Homework
(Dinosaurs)

Production of this Flying Rhino book was assisted by Friends of the Children, a
nonprofit organization dedicated to providing to at-risk youth a one-on-one, caring
relationship with a positive adult role model. If you agree such relationships are
fundamental to a child's physical, emotional and spiritual well-being, and want to help
Friends of the Children, please call (503) 275-9675.

Library of Congress Catalog Number 94-078337
ISBN 1-883772-04-4
Copyright 1994 by Flying Rhino Productions, Inc.
All rights reserved.
No portion of this book may be reproduced without written permission
from Flying Rhino Productions, Inc.
Book design by Heather Corcoran, Portland Trail Blazers
Printing by Bridgetown Printing, Portland, Oregon
Binding by Lincoln and Allen, Portland, Oregon
Color separations by Wy'east, Portland, Oregon

 This book printed on recycled paper using soy-based inks.

Dear Readers,

In the pages that follow, you will read about Dewey and how, through basketball, he took on an important personal challenge: he learned to believe in himself. His is a lesson that we all can learn from – on the basketball court, in school, at the dinner table or on the playground.

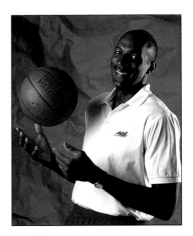

As chairman for the BASIC (Blazers Avia Scholastic Improvements Concepts) program for the past seven years, I believe in the importance of learning to read. Reading helps us understand our world and learn valuable lessons about life through the experiences of others.

This book is a great way to start learning. And don't forget that, after all, "shrews *can* hoop!"

Sincerely,

Clyde Drexler
#22

Clyde Drexler

shrew (shroo) n. 1. Any of various small, chiefly insectivorous mammals of the family Soricidae, having a long, pointed nose and small, often poorly developed eyes. Sometimes called "shrewmouse." Can, at times, be found watching cartoons and munching on chocolate chip cookies.

Once upon a time there was a shrew named Dewey. Dewey was like most other shrews that lived in the forest. He was small, fuzzy and very quiet. There was one thing, however, different about Dewey. He loved to play basketball.

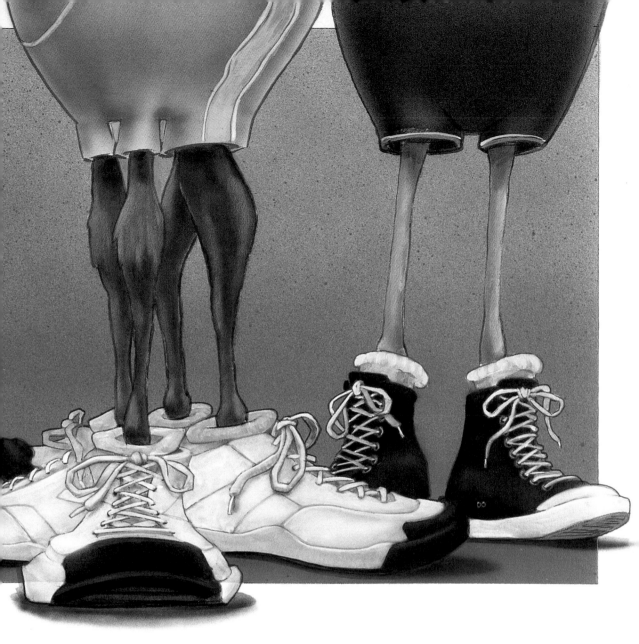

Every morning Dewey went to play basketball with the rest of the forest creatures. Even though he was the size of a thimble, Dewey stretched his little muscles and tried to warm up with the other players. But he noticed that instead of playing hoops, he spent most of his time trying to keep from being stepped on.

All of the other animals towered above him like the giant Douglas Firs that grew in the forest.

"Hello Mr. Bear...do you mind if I shoot baskets with you?" The bear's eyes narrowed as he looked down, down, down at Dewey. He wiped the slobber from his mouth and growled...

Basketball's a game of strength and sheer muscle,
it's not about quickness, jumping or hustle.
I laugh at the players I knock to the floor,
if you run into me you'll hustle no more.
Every rebound that bounces up high in the air
is mine, only mine, I never will share.
(If I squish you to get it, I really don't care.)

You're too small and too frail. . . too feeble and weak,
your chances of playing this game are quite bleak.
So scurry on home, before you suffer a bruise,
or become a small grease spot under my shoes.

It's really quite simple, here's the straight poop:
this game is for giants...

Shrews can not hoop!

Dewey decided it would be best to leave
the bear alone. So he wiped a big glob of
bear drool off his shoulder and scurried over to
a moose who was busy bouncing a ball on his antlers.

Dewey cleared his throat and squeaked, "Hello Mr. Moose, do you mind
if I warm up with you?"

The moose looked down, down, down at Dewey and rolled his big eyes
back in his head.

He blared...

> You must be quite tall to be good at this sport,
> and, as you well know, you are shorter than short.
> I know I sound cruel and I'm being a grouch,
> but I've seen taller dust bunnies under my couch.
> This isn't your sport... you'll only get beat,
> try it again when you've grown a few feet.
>
> Let me tell you small fry, here's the straight scoop:
> there's no way out here that. . .

Shrews get to hoop!

With that, the moose
snorted at Dewey and
trotted to the other
end of the court.

ZZOOOOOMMMM!!!

Dewey was thrown up into the air as a rabbit ran by him. He whirled and twirled and landed with a thud. "Hey Mr. Rabbit, do you mind if I warm up with you guys?"

"You want to warm up with us?" giggled the rabbit. "I wouldn't mind except that you couldn't keep up with us." Another rabbit pointed at Dewey, "You've gotta be kidding Shrewmouse, you move like there's a big wad of gum stuck to the sole of your shoes."

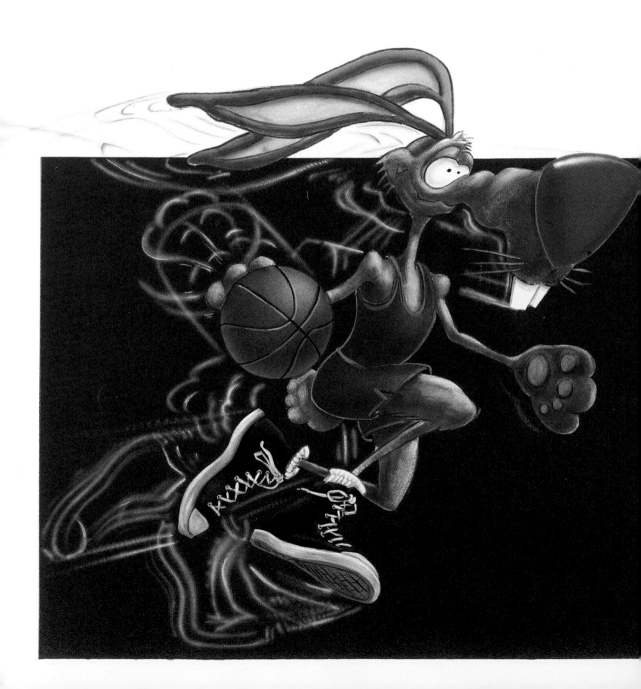

Speed is the key to playing this game,
with quickness like ours we'll be Hall of Fame.
We really must say, we hope you don't play,
you run like molasses on a cold winter day.

You'll never play ball, or be one of the group,
it's really quite simple...

Shrews stink at hoop!

Ha Ha Ha Ha Ha Ha Ha Ha Ha Ha Ha Ha!

It was the rat brothers, and they were laughing at Dewey.

Dewey gave them a glare. "What's so funny, you guys?"

"You are! We've never seen anyone so silly," replied Stinky Rat.
(Everyone called the oldest brother Stinky because...well, because he
was stinky.)

Dewey crossed his arms and growled, "What makes you rats think you're
better than me?"

"There's a reason they call it 'Ratball' ya know."

We're not very big... we're really not quick,
we play in a way that makes everyone sick.
We poke and we tease, we talk lots of trash,
we spit and we scream, we cause quite a rash.
Some of the players say that we're rude,
we simply call it... a slight attitude.
Your problem, dear Shrew, isn't your size.
You're just too darn sweet to bring home the prize.
You send flowers to momma and don't burp at dinner.
You're not mean enough to be a real winner.

So listen to us for a bit of advice. . .

Shrews can not HOOP. . . they're just too darn nice!

Dewey was tired of all the rats' nonsense so he scooted over to the
sideline where the players were picking teams for the game.

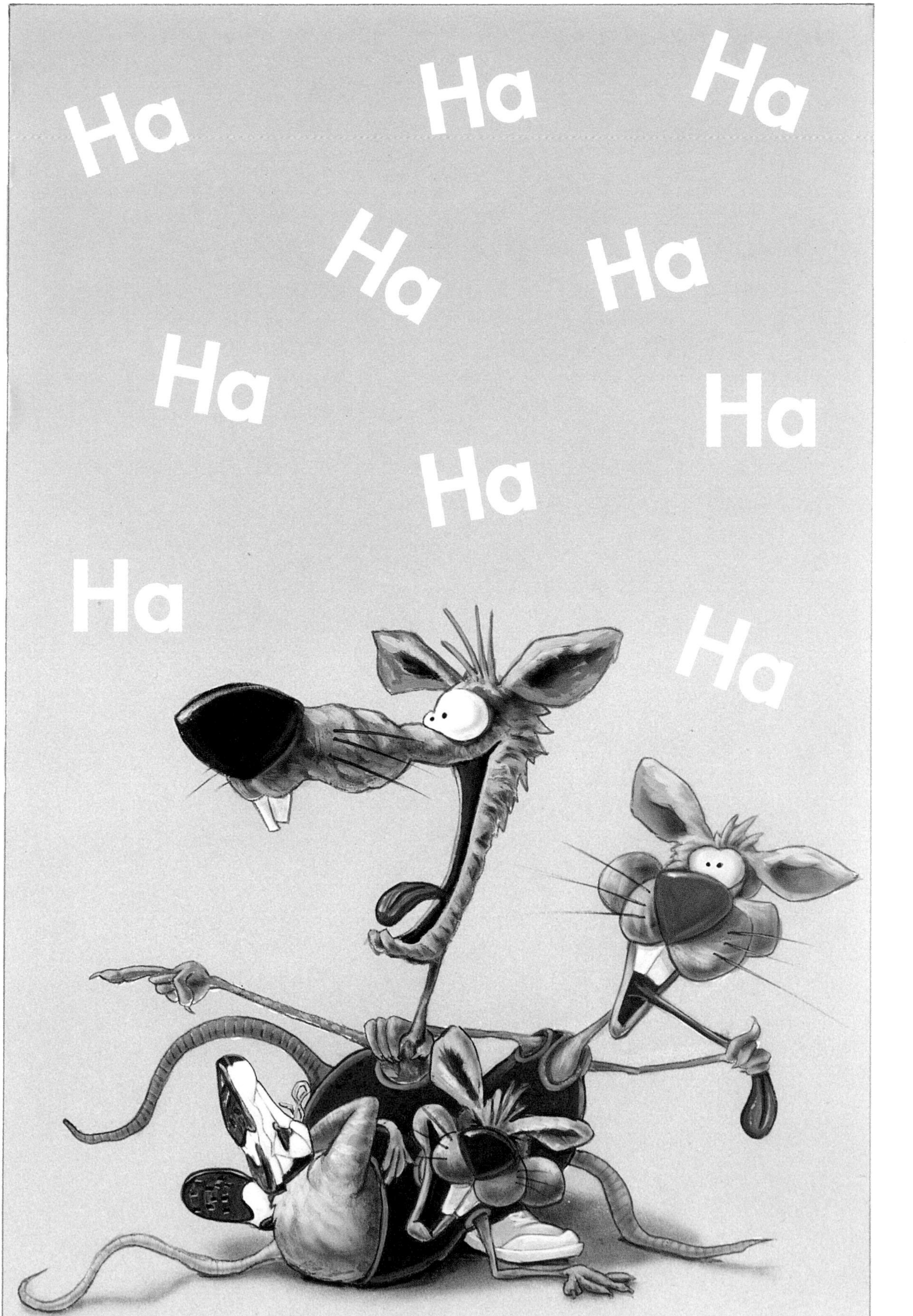
Ha
Ha
Ha
Ha
Ha
Ha
Ha
Ha
Ha
Ha

As long as everyone could remember, Bear and Moose had always been team captains. Nobody knows exactly why Bear and Moose were always the team captains. (One day, a few years ago, Squirrel asked Bear if he could be captain and Bear ate him. Since that day, Bear and Moose have always been captains.)

"I pick Rabbit," said Bear. "I pick Rat," answered Moose. "Beaver.... I pick Duck...Rabbit... Deer... Skunk..."

Dewey looked about in horror as he realized that there was only room for one more player. There were still two players left standing on the sidelines. The two worst players in the forest were waiting to see who would be picked. Just Dewey and... Seymour Snail.

Now, Dewey wasn't very fast but he could run circles around Seymour. Dewey couldn't jump very high but he could jump right over Seymour's shell. Not to mention, Seymour left a really gross trail of slime wherever he went. Dewey thought to himself that he might actually get picked.

(I mean if you had to pick between a cute little fuzzy guy like Dewey or a slimy gross gooey gastropod like Seymour, wouldn't you pick Dewey?)

But then Dewey noticed something written on the basketball in blue crayon..."PROPERTY OF SEYMOUR SNAIL."

Dewey smacked his forehead. "This can't be happening," he thought.

Moose leaned into Dewey's face. "I pick Seymour so we can use his ball."

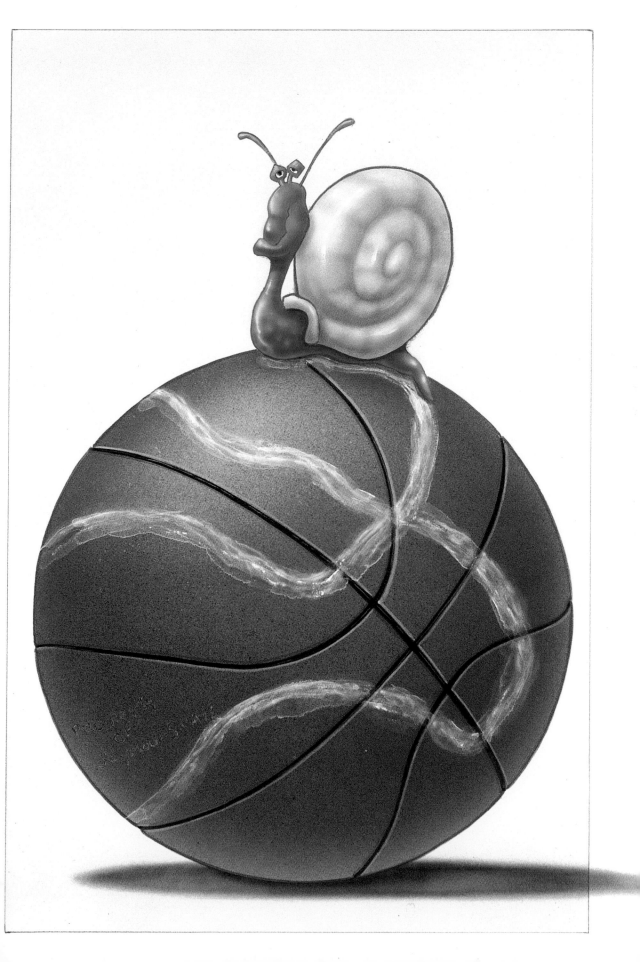

Dewey turned away quickly so that no one would see the tears welling up in his eyes. As he ran away, he heard Moose yell, "Hey, somebody wipe the ball off and let's get the game going!"

Maybe... Shrews can't hoop??

OF COURSE YOU CAN....BELIEVE IN YOURSELF...TRY YOUR HARDEST...BE POSITIVE..YOU CAN DO IT...OF COURSE YOU CAN....

Dewey wandered around for hours. He walked all the way down to the big river where he found a rock to sit on. He pulled off his sneakers and stretched his little toes. "I'm a failure. I'm too small and too slow ever to do anything important." He stared at his reflection in the river. He sat and stared for hours until he noticed a large river turtle swimming by.

"Hello there!" yelled the turtle.

Dewey just sighed.

"What seems to be the problem, my small fuzzy friend?"

"I'm a failure," Dewey said. "All I have ever wanted is to be a great basketball player. . . but all of the other players are so much bigger and faster and stronger than me. Every time I try to play, they just laugh at me."

"Come here little guy. . . I want to share a story with you."

The turtle lifted Dewey up onto his knee and put his arm around the little shrewmouse.

"A long time ago, when I was just a pup, everyone made fun of how slow I was. It took me all day just to tie my shoes.

"There was this annoying rabbit. He always made fun of me. So one day. . . ya know what I did? I went right up to that long-eared trouble maker and I challenged him to a race! Well, everyone thought that was the funniest thing they had ever heard... a turtle challenging a rabbit to a race.

"I knew that it would be hard to beat the rabbit in a race. So I spent many days training and practicing. I told myself over and over again, 'I can beat that rabbit. . . I know I can beat that rabbit!'

"The day of the big race finally arrived and you know what? I went out and beat that rabbit. It's really quite simple. You can do anything you want to do. Nobody can stop you from making your dreams come true. If you practice real hard and believe in yourself, you can do anything that you want to."

With that, the turtle lowered Dewey to the ground and gave him a little wink. He waved a goodbye and swam off into the river.

Dewey spent all afternoon thinking about what the turtle had told him. "Nobody is going to stop me from accomplishing my dream," he declared. He would get up early in the morning and start practicing.

That night Dewey took a warm bubble bath and pulled on his favorite pajamas. (The ones with the fuzzy feet and the trapdoor.) He chugged a big mug of hot cocoa and climbed into bed where he fell quickly asleep.

COURSE YOU CAN....BELIEVE IN YOURSELF...TRY YOUR HARDEST...BE POSITIVE...YOU CAN DO IT...OF COURSE YOU CAN....BELIE

The next morning Dewey gathered up a jump rope, some weights and a basketball. He took a deep breath and began practicing. . .

He worked on his dribbling and ball handling.

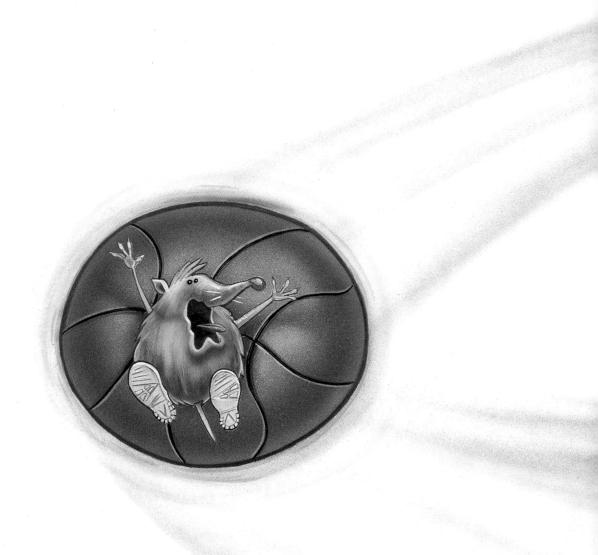

(Most of the time it looked like the ball was handling Dewey.)

He worked on his jump shot.

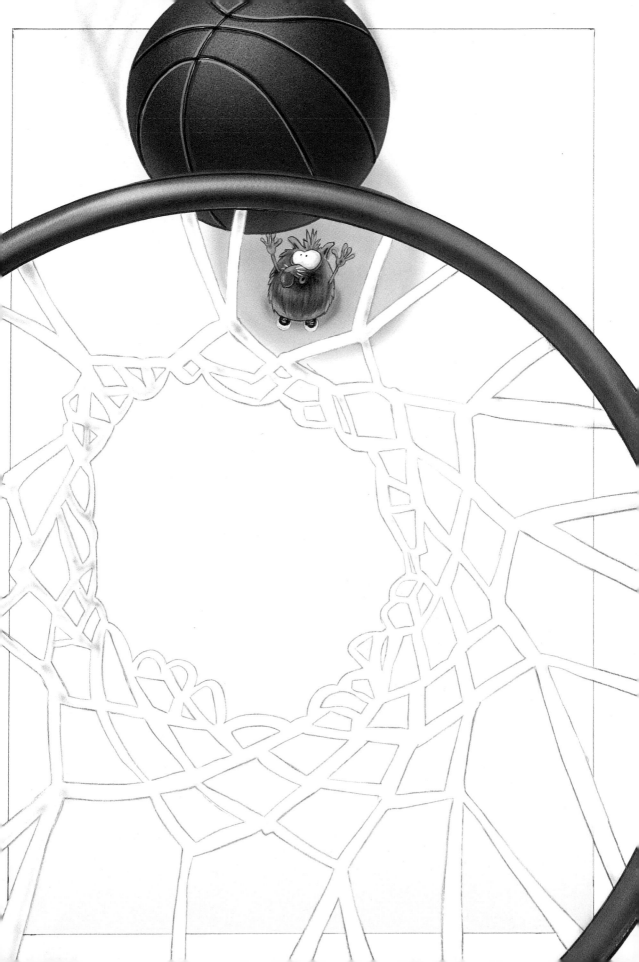

Dewey practiced for hours, days and months on end. He became
very good at dribbling and shooting. He shot from the meadow. . .
SWOOSH, SWISH, SWOOSH! He shot from the big mossy stump. . .
SWISH, SWOOSH, SWISH! He could even make baskets from
across the pond. He had become a very good basketball player
indeed. It was time to go back to the games and prove to everyone
that shrews can hoop.

Dewey arrived at the court just as the teams were being picked.

He was in luck. Where was Seymour Snail?

Dewey looked about and Seymour was nowhere to be found. Then he remembered it was Thursday. Seymour always had his tuba lessons on Thursday.

The tiny shrew's heart raced as he realized that he might actually get a chance to play today. Moose leaned down, down, down to Dewey's face and snorted, "OK. . . I pick you, Shrew."

Dewey jumped in the air with glee. . . falling flat on his face.

Moose just stared at Dewey and sighed.

"I Pick you... Shrew "

The ball was tossed up in the air. Bear jumped up and started to tip it to rabbit. . . when out of nowhere, Dewey shot into the sky. He gave a little growl and tapped the ball away from Bear.

This caught everyone so off guard that they froze like statues.

They just stood there looking at Dewey. How could a tiny shrew steal the ball from Bear?

Dewey grabbed the ball and dribbled toward the basket. He pumped his little legs as fast and as hard as he could. He felt the pounding of the other animals chasing after him and he heard Stinky Rat yell, "Step on him...step on him."

Dewey knew it was time to make his move.

Dewey planted his little foot just behind the free throw line and jumped with all of his might. He soared up, up, up into the sky, higher than he had ever jumped before. He sprang off Moose's antlers. . . hopped over rabbit and shot toward the rim. He brought the ball back behind his head and slam dunked like no rodent has ever slam dunked before.

All of the forest creatures stared in amazement as Dewey hung from the rim. And then. . . ever so gently. . . Bear reached up and grabbed Dewey. He lowered the little shrewmouse down to the ground and cleared his throat.

In a deep grizzly voice he said. . .

We've acted just awful, really quite cruel,
I feel like a heel, I feel like a fool.
It isn't our place to tell others they're wrong,
instead we should try to help them along.
My small fuzzy friend, you've shown us all,
you don't have to be big or fast to play ball.
What you need is inside, it comes from your heart,
your desire and dreams will set you apart.

We've been immature and caused quite a fuss.
Today, Dewey Shrew, you're bigger than us.

With that, the bear grabbed Dewey's tiny paw and shook. Dewey's teeth clattered and his arm felt like it would come apart from his little body. But it was the best feeling he had ever felt. He was one of the gang. He was now a real basketball player.

The entire group of animals sat down in the shade of an ancient fir tree. They giggled and they laughed and they shared a cool drink. It was the day that everyone learned. . .

Shrews really can hoop!

SHEILA LUCAS

Douglas Kelly & Ray Nelson, Jr.

Doug Kelly doesn't know anything about basketball. But what he lacks in basketball knowledge he more than makes up for in artistic talent. Doug studied art at Art Center College of Design in Pasadena, California, and has worked on five children's books to date. He enjoys looking for his golf balls on golf courses all over Oregon, as well as spending time with his friends Victoria and Toonces the Cat.

Ever since Ray Nelson was dropped on his head as a small child, he has loved to draw goofy pictures and write silly stories. He currently spends his days writing and illustrating books for Flying Rhino Productions, Inc. in Portland, Oregon. Ray also loves to play basketball. He actually played small college basketball and today still holds a record for most personal fouls committed in a season. (Pretty amazing since he only played 20 seconds a game.) In his spare time, he loves to hang out with his wife, Theresa, his daughter, Alexandria and his two hundred pound dog, Molly the Great Dane. Ray doesn't have much spare time, however, because he is constantly cleaning up the drool left behind by a two hundred pound dog and a two year old daughter.

Special Thanks

Marta Monetti, Amy Westlund, Julie Mohr, Mike McLane, Norm Myhr, Sharon Higdon, Melody Stafford, Jim Taylor, Chris Nelson, Jeff Nuss and Ben Adams.